Stupid Trousers

SUSAN GATES

Illustrated by Martin Remphry

OXFORD
UNIVERSITY PRESS

OXFORD
UNIVERSITY PRESS

Great Clarendon Street, Oxford OX2 6DP

Oxford University Press is a department of the University of Oxford.
It furthers the University's objective of excellence in research, scholarship,
and education by publishing worldwide in

Oxford   New York

Auckland   Cape Town   Dar es Salaam   Hong Kong   Karachi
Kuala Lumpur   Madrid   Melbourne   Mexico City   Nairobi
New Delhi   Shanghai   Taipei   Toronto

With offices in

Argentina   Austria   Brazil   Chile   Czech Republic   France   Greece
Guatemala   Hungary   Italy   Japan   Poland   Portugal   Singapore
South Korea   Switzerland   Thailand   Turkey   Ukraine   Vietnam

Oxford is a registered trade mark of Oxford University Press
in the UK and in certain other countries

British Library Cataloguing in Publication Data
Data available

ISBN-13: 978-0-19-917966-4
ISBN-10: 0-19-917966-2

1 3 5 7 9 10 8 6 4 2

Available in packs
Stage 10 More Stories A Pack of 6:
ISBN-13: 978-0-19-917963-3; ISBN-10: 0-19-917963-8
Stage 10 More Stories A Class Pack:
ISBN-13: 978-0-19-917970-1; ISBN-10: 0-19-917970-0
Guided Reading Cards also available:
ISBN-13: 978-0-19-917972-5; ISBN-10: 0-19-917972-7

Cover artwork by Martin Remphry
Photograph of Susan Gates © Pauline Holbrook

Printed in China by Imago

'No!' shouted Ross. 'No way!'

His big brother Lee said, 'Go on. Try them on.'

'No way!' shouted Ross again.

Ross was going to be a pageboy at his big sister Kerry's wedding. And he had just seen the clothes he had to wear.

'I hate them!' he shouted.

He hated the frilly shirt. He hated the red bow tie. But, most of all, he hated the trousers. They were red too. They were made of velvet.

'Those stupid trousers are too long!' Ross shouted. 'They'll trip me up. Everyone will laugh at me.'

'No, they won't,' said Lee.

'Yes, they will! And you can shut up. You're stupid as well!'

'No, I'm not stupid. You're stupid!'

Kerry had come into the room.

'Stop saying rude things to your brother,' she told Lee. 'He's only little.'

'It's not fair,' said Lee. 'He can say rude things to me. He can say whatever he likes. But I can't say them back to him. Just because he's *only little*.'

Lee stamped out of the room.

'And I'm not wearing those stupid trousers!' yelled Ross. 'They'll trip me up. Everyone will laugh at me!'

He stamped out of the room too.

'Oh dear,' said Kerry.

She looked at the trousers.

'Ross is right. They are a bit too long,' she said to herself.

FRAGILE

7

She got out a needle and thread. She got some scissors. Snip, snip, she cut a bit off the trousers. Then she sewed them up again.

'There, that's short enough,' she thought.

She left the trousers on the back of the chair.

All that day Ross was in a really bad
mood. He banged doors. He stamped
around the house.

He hated that frilly shirt. He hated
the red bow tie. But, most of all, he
hated those stupid trousers.

'They'll trip me up,' he told Lee. 'In a church! In front of all those people. Everyone will laugh at me.'

Just thinking about it made him squirm.

'No way!' he told Lee. 'I'm not going to be a pageboy. I'm not going to the wedding. I'm going to run away!'

That night Lee couldn't sleep.
Sometimes he got mad with his
little brother. But, really, he quite
liked him. He didn't want him to
run away.

'What can I do?' he thought.
He couldn't worry Mum. She
was busy with the wedding. She
had enough on her mind.

Suddenly, *Ping!* An idea popped into his head.

He slipped out of bed. It was very dark. He listened. The house was still and quiet. He crept downstairs like a burglar.

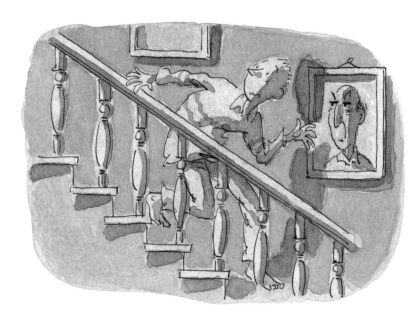

Creak! What was that noise? Only the stairs. Did it wake Mum up? He listened.

'It's OK. No one heard,' he told himself.

He crept into the living room. He looked around.

'There they are!'

There were the trousers on a chair. Just where Kerry had left them. Then he saw a silver flash in the dark. It was the scissors.

'Great!' he thought. 'Just what I need.'

He picked up the scissors. Then snip, snip, he cut a big bit off each trouser leg.

'That's short enough now,' he thought.

He felt really pleased with himself.

He left the trousers on the chair. Then he went back to bed and fell fast asleep.

Someone else in the house
was still wide awake.

It was Ross.

He didn't want to run away. It was
far too scary. And, anyway, he didn't
know where to run to.

But what else could he do?

15

He could put up with the frilly shirt. He could even stand the bow tie. But he just couldn't stand those stupid, long trousers.

Then, *Ping!* An idea popped into his head.

He slipped out of bed. He listened. He couldn't hear a sound.

'Good, they're all asleep,' he thought. He tiptoed downstairs.

It was spooky in the dark. There were big shadows on the walls. One looked like a monster with long fingers, trying to grab him.

'Aaargh!'

Something brushed against his leg.
Something furry.

He nearly jumped out of his skin.

'Miaow!' it said.

'Phew!' said Ross. 'Is that you,
Tiddles? I thought you were a monster!'

He tiptoed into the living room.

He had to find those trousers. At last,
he saw them. They were hanging on
the chair, where Lee had left them.

He picked up the scissors.

He didn't dare put the light on. It was hard to see what he was doing. But that didn't stop him. Snip, snip. He cut two, great big bits off each trouser leg.

'That's short enough,' he thought.
'They won't trip me up now.'
He didn't have to run away.
He felt really pleased with himself.

He left the trousers on the chair. He
went back to bed and fell fast asleep.

Next morning was the day of the
wedding. Mum got up before everyone
else. She had lots to do. She went
downstairs humming a little tune.

'Aaaaaaaaaaargh!'

A terrible scream rang through the house. It shook the windows. It rattled the doors. It woke everyone up.

Mum had just found the trousers.

Everyone was shouting at once.
It was a terrible din.

'How did they get so short!' yelled
Kerry.

'Don't ask me,' said Lee and Ross,
both at the same time.

Kerry was really mad. She was
waving the trousers around.

Only, they weren't trousers any more. They were very short, red, velvet shorts.

'Never mind how it happened,' said Mum. 'Let's all calm down. Try them on, Ross. They might still look all right.'

'No way! No way! No way!' Ross started yelling.

But Kerry looked really dangerous.
So Ross had to try them on.

Kerry and Mum and Lee all stared at
Ross in his tiny, red velvet shorts.

'Do you think they look all right?'
asked Mum.

'He looks quite sweet,' said Kerry.

'I don't want to look sweet!' howled Ross.

'He does look sweet, doesn't he?' Mum agreed.

'Oh no,' thought Lee. 'They're going to make him wear them!'

He had to do something, fast!

Then, *Ping!* An idea popped into his head.

'Look at his legs,' he said to Mum and Kerry. 'They look really stupid! They're white and skinny. They're horrible. They're like two white sticks!'

Ross opened his mouth. He was going to yell, 'Stop saying rude things about my legs!'

But then he understood. He understood
that Lee was trying to *help* him!

So he said, 'Lee's right. My legs look
horrible.'

'I told you,' said Lee. 'And he's got
scabby knees as well. Uuurgh! They'll
make people sick!'

'I have! I have!' agreed Ross. 'Look at them, Mum! They're horrible. They're so scabby, they even make *me* sick!'

Mum was thinking.

'Lee's right,' she said, at last. 'Those trousers won't do at all.'

'He'll have to wear something else,' said Kerry.

'Great!' said Lee and Ross both at the same time.

So Ross went to the wedding in a pair of his own trousers.

'Thank you, Lee!' said Ross. 'Thanks for being so rude to me. Thank you! Thank you! Thank you! You saved me from those stupid trousers.'

'That's all right,' said Lee. 'Any time.'

He couldn't help giving a big grin.

It's not every day your little brother gives you a great big Thank You. Just when you've been really rude to him.

And all because of a pair of stupid trousers.

About the author

I have a confession to make.
I borrowed this story. I
borrowed it from my dad,
Ken Robinson. Years ago,
when he was a teacher, he
used to tell this story to his
class. One day, he told it to
me. And I've remembered
it all this time.

Before I wrote it, I rang him up. I said,
'Dad, you know that story you used to tell?
The one about the trousers? Is it all right if
I borrow it?' And he said, 'What story?'
He'd forgotten all about it!